Also by
James Aldridge in Piccolo
The Marvellous Mongolian

James Aldridge
The Flying 19

illustrated by Raymond Briggs

Piccolo Pan Books
London and Sydney

First published in Great Britain 1966 by
Hamish Hamilton Children's Books Ltd
This edition published 1979 by Pan Books Ltd,
Cavaye Place, London SW10 9PG
© James Aldridge 1966
Illustrations © Raymond Briggs 1966
ISBN 0 330 25634 3
Made and printed in Great Britain by
Cox and Wyman Ltd, London, Reading and Fakenham

to Sister Morell
and all the other Sisters and Nurses
of Lilian Ward for children,
St Thomas's Hospital

Chapter 1

IT was a cold day in November and everything was normal in London. The traffic was jammed everywhere, from Battersea to Bermondsey. Everybody was late for work and school, everybody was angry and upset.

The Chief Deputy Decontroller of London Buses, who naturally travelled to work by Underground, came out at Piccadilly and saw a hundred buses stuck fast in Piccadilly.

"Hello, Joe," he said to the nearest driver of a No. 19 bus. "How are things today?"

"Same as usual," Joe said. Joe was an old London bus driver who smoked a pipe and when he said something important he puffed twice on his pipe, *pum pum*, which he did now.

ow late are you today, Joe?" the
D (Chief Deputy Decontroller) said.

"Hour. Hour-and-a-half." Joe went
pum pum on his pipe.

"I suppose Bob, Jim and Andy are also
late?"

"Right," Joe said. "And it's getting
worse."

"And it's terribly disgusting," someone
shouted at the CDD.

It was a passenger who had rolled down
the window and had put his head out. He
was all covered in white hair and looked
like a sunflower, he had so many freckles.
He was very angry.

"My dinner will be worried," he
shouted. "My wife will be spoiled. You
ought to be ashamed of yourself, the way
you run these buses."

"Now, Professor," someone said and
pulled his head back into the bus and
rolled up the window. "You're not going

home to your dinner, you're on your way to work."

The person who spoke was the coloured conductress called Sidi which is short for Siderone. She was a strict conductress and took no nonsense from anyone except the Professor. She sang all day.

"Don't be silly," the Professor said to Sidi.

Sidi laughed.

"I don't believe you," the Professor said angrily. He was always saying he didn't believe you, it, that, this, or them. He was so absent-minded. He never knew where he was, or whether he was coming or going, or whether it was morning or evening, or which day it was or what he had to do next, and sometimes he didn't even know who he was; but he knew everything else. He was the cleverest man in England.

The bus moved an inch and stopped

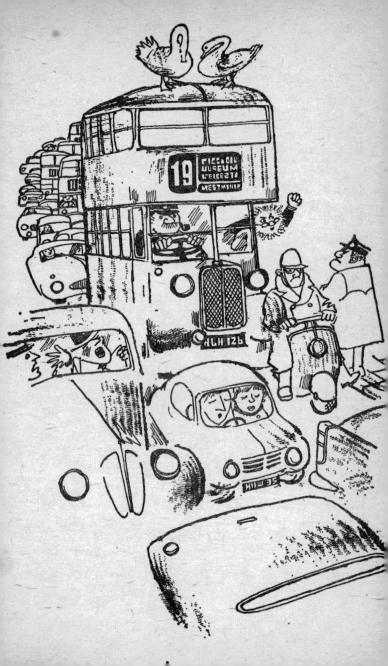

again. That was the second inch in half-an-hour. Two swans landed on the roof and began to clean their dirty necks. Everybody became a little more angry.

"How terribly disgusting," the Professor said again. "It's all terribly disgusting. Every day it gets more terribly disgusting."

Everybody in the bus said the same thing.

Jix and Jax were twins, and usually they quarrelled about everything because they were not two girls or two boy twins but a boy and a girl. They were on their way to school in Piccadilly and every morning they were later and later and got more and more detentions, punishments, lines, reprimands, homeworks.

"We'll be twenty-one minutes late," Jix said.

"We'll be twenty-four minutes late," Jax argued.

They began to argue about it angrily, and finally Sidi the conductress said to them:

"Now listen, Jix and Jax, no quarrelling on my bus. Only the Professor knows how late you will be, so ask him and stop quarrelling."

The Professor knew everything so they asked him how late they would be today and the Professor looked at the traffic which was still piling up, and at the date on the newspaper, and he said, "Twenty-two and three-quarter minutes."

This made the Professor so angry that

he rapped on the window and said to the driver:

"Tom!"

"Name's Joe," corrected Joe and went *pum pum*.

"Yes, that's what I said, Joe. Can't you get around this traffic somehow? Go up on the footpath . . ."

"Can't do that!" Joe said. He was always a man of few words.

"But I'll be terribly, terribly late! I've got to give an important lecture after lunch."

"Sorry, Professor," Joe said, "but you'd need a bloomin' flying bus to get through this lot."

"Then why on earth haven't you got a flying bus?" the Professor said, and put his head out of the window again and shouted at the CDD. "Well? That's your job, isn't it? Why haven't you got a flying bus on this route?"

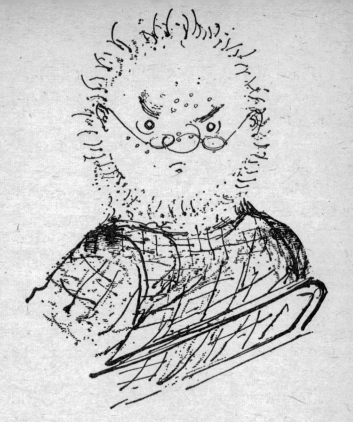

The CDD smiled. "Now you know very well, Professor," he said, "that nobody's invented a flying bus yet."

"Why not?" the Professor demanded.

"Yes!" everybody on the bus said. "Why not?"

They all looked at Sidi the conductress.

"Don't blame me," Sidi said. "I couldn't invent one."

"Why don't you invent one, Professor?" Jix and Jax said.

"Me? I haven't time for that sort of nonsense."

"Nobody could invent a flying double-decker London bus," everybody else said. "That's impossible."

"Impossible?" The Professor was furious. "Nothing is impossible. Of course I'll invent one. I can't be late like this all the time."

"It's impossible," everybody said, and Sidi sang, "Im*possi*ble, im*possi*ble, im*possi*ble."

The Professor was furious. "Don't you dare say that awful word to me again. Of course I'll invent a flying double-decker London bus. Who said it was impossible? Who said that?"

He turned around and glared. Nobody dared look at the Professor's sunflower face, nobody would dare argue with him, not even Sidi. And that was how the flying double-decker London bus No. 19 was invented.

Naturally there were difficulties. The Professor forgot all about it for a long time and one day he remembered that he had to invent something but couldn't remember what it was, and he said to his little wife who looked just like a lively little female sunflower: "I've got to invent something that flies, Esmeralda. Do you have any idea what it is, please?"

"You never told me about it, my dear," she said.

"Didn't I? Well, it was something silly."

"A flying saucer?" his wife suggested.

"No, no."

"A flying house-mouse?"

"No, it was a flying tea cup. No, it was

a flying museum. No, no, no, no!" the Professor said angrily, and thought for a moment.

"Perhaps it was a flying Professor," Esmeralda said slyly, because she loved to play little jokes on him.

"Of course it was," he said. "You are always right, my dear."

Esmeralda was alarmed. "Really, Andrew, you're not . . ."

"No, no, no. Not myself. It's a bus. What would I do without you?" Then he leaned over and kissed his wife on the left elbow instead of the cheek because he was already thinking of the formula: Cxa (A–BO*m" x ss334) by (A–B 442*÷ ddXy) multiplied by 2 minus (x-z41re# r2 x 4 ÷ ½ — 7@?/) = 1.

That was how the flying double-decker London bus was first invented.

It flew very well. When Joe was testing it around the bus station he passed by a man eating ham and eggs for breakfast on the second floor, and the man was so stunned to see a bus outside his second-storey window that he swore he would never touch a drop of ham and eggs again.

Chapter 2

OF course everybody wanted to travel on the Flying 19 because it simply flew over all the traffic jams and always arrived on time, everywhere. But Joe and Sidi had their regulars, which Sidi sang about every morning: "*Regulars, regoolars, regularos . . .*" The real regulars were Jix and Jax and the Professor and Mrs Nuttall, a young lady char who was going to have a baby.

Jix and Jax argued every day when they got on the bus. "We will be two minutes early today," Jix said. "Four minutes," Jax said.

Of course they always asked the Professor to settle their arguments and this time the Professor said: "Three minutes."

But Jix and Jax never really quarrelled. Their arguments were usually very serious, such as who would be first man on the moon—an American or a Russian. Only the Professor could possibly know the answer to that and when, after a long time of very hot argument about it, they asked him, the Professor replied impatiently: "That's just silly. It's not going to be a Russian *or* an American."

"Who will it be then, Professor?"

"A Miridon will be the first man on the moon," the Professor said.

"A Miridon?" the twins asked together, very surprised. They had never heard of a Miridon.

"Miridon is a small country in the small part of Central Asia," the Professor said. "Now be quiet. I'll forget what I was thinking about if you keep on bothering me like this."

The No. 19 didn't fly all the time, of

course, only when all the traffic was jammed up. One by one it picked up its regulars as it came from Tooting Bec through Wandsworth and Battersea; but every morning when it got to Battersea Bridge there was the usual queue of traffic for miles and miles, all the way to Piccadilly in fact.

"Take off, Joe," everybody shouted excitedly. "We'll be late."

But Joe was very patient and went *pum pum* on his pipe. He had to be sure. He always had to be sure. He was very reliable. But there was obviously no way out, and he began to hear the Professor boiling behind him, so he pulled down a big switch called the "Atomatic Adjuster" which made adjustments for everything: wind, ice, snow, fog, flying saucers, helicopters, ducks, drakes and angry aeroplane pilots who hated the flying bus. Every time they saw it they tried to spit

on it. Joe sometimes had a hard time dodging them.

"Hold tight, please," Sidi said politely. "This is not a stop. We're going UP."

Joe went *pum pum* on his pipe and the bus rose like a bird.

"There goes the Flying 19," everybody below them shouted.

Everybody waved. Everybody jammed up in the traffic below was envious of the

regularos on the Flying 19. Of course Joe had to obey the London Transport Rules and Regulations, so he flew low at all the Request stops. When the bell rang to stop he would bring the bus down in an empty space which everybody below made for them, because everybody loved the Flying 19.

"Hold tight, please!" Sidi ordered again, and UP they went. "Fares, please," she said then.

The fare on the Flying 19 was a halfpenny dearer than on the non-flying 19s because London Transport, who run all the buses, couldn't allow people to arrive on time without charging them extra for it, could they?

At Piccadilly, where Jix and Jax went to a special school to stop boy and girl twins quarrelling, they said goodbye to Sidi and waved to Joe, who would never take his hands off the steering wheel but went *pum pum* on his pipe, and off they went quarrelling madly about the depth of the sea at Kamchatka.

Of course there was the usual miles and miles of traffic jam at Piccadilly, so Joe took No. 19 UP and flew as gracefully as a blind swan around Eros, and down Shaftesbury Avenue where all the typists and hairdressers and people who worked on all the first floors waved to Flying 19 as it flew by.

It was a very happy bus, and Sidi sang more and more.

The most important stop was for the Professor, who got out near the British Museum. Sidi would get off the bus and point the Professor in the direction he would have to go, so that he would not forget. Then Joe would go *pum pum* and drive or fly the bus for the rest of the morning.

At twelve o'clock they came in to the

Bus Garage at Battersea Bridge, and that was the end of their day, because they had started work at 6.03 a.m. in the morning. Joe went home to his cat and dog and whistling canary, and Sidi went home to all her dark sisters who loved her very much because she was the first flying conductress in the world.

But it was not always so easy on Flying 19. They sometimes had troubles . . .

Chapter 3

IT was foggy. All London transport had stopped. Even the Underground had stopped. Dogs got lost and birds refused to fly. It was a pea souper, which went on for days.

The Professor was very angry because he had to give an important lecture to twenty-four Greek professors who were waiting for him at the British Museum.

The Professor rang up London Transport.

"Where's my bus?" he shouted at them.

"What bus are you talking about, Professor?" the Official said calmly.

"What bus!" the Professor repeated angrily. "What do you mean?" And the Professor said some terrible things.

The Official was very calm, and as usual pretended to know nothing at all of what the Professor was talking about until he

had made the Professor good and mad, and then he said very nicely:

"Oh, you mean the Flying 19."

The Professor said unspeakable things to the Official.

"I'm afraid all routes are cancelled to-day, Professor," the Official said very happily because they always felt happiest at London Transport when they were cancelling buses right, left and centre. "Too much fog."

"But the Flying 19 doesn't care about fog," the Professor shouted angrily. "It can go anywhere at any time. It has got a special Atomatic Regulator on it which regulates for everything. If you don't get that bus around here immediately," the Professor threatened, "I shall invent a formula for turning all London Transport Officials into blue and green Unofficials, even on the telephone."

Of course the Official saw reason

immediately and telephoned Battersea Garage and told Joe, who had walked to the Garage, to take out the Flying 19 on the usual route.

"I suppose you can manage," the Official said.

"I'll manage," Joe said. *Pum pum*.

Joe knew his No. 19 route so well he didn't even need to see it so he took UP the Flying 19 very confidently.

It was just as well the Professor had insisted on the bus that day, because something even more important happened. First Joe picked up the Professor, flying blind of course to the Professor's stop in Clapham. He was only one foot out when he landed at the stop. Then he picked up the twins, Jix and Jax, who were quarrelling that morning about the number of birds in the world, a very important subject. Jix said there were four hundred thousand million, and Jax said there were three hundred and twenty-one trillion. They went on arguing very angrily about this as they hopped on the bus.

Joe was just about to take off when Sidi, who hated the fog and never sang on foggy days, heard Mrs Nuttall, the young lady char, and her husband hurrying down the street.

"Hang on," Mr Nuttall shouted to Sidi.

Sidi pushed the bell again and Joe landed the bus.

"Come on," Sidi said firmly. "I can't wait here all day."

"I'm sorry, luv," Mrs Nuttall said breathlessly as she got on, "but I think my baby is going to be born any minute and I must get to St. Thomas's Hospital very quickly."

"But we don't go anywhere near St. Thomas's Hospital," Sidi said.

"I know, luv," Mrs Nuttall said. "But

it's too foggy for the ambulance, and I think I'm going to have my new baby very, very soon, so couldn't you swing off a bit and drop me off at St. Thomas's?"

Sidi was a very sympathetic person and she helped Mrs Nuttall into one of the seats and told the twins to stop arguing and then knocked on the window and said to Joe:

"Joe! Can you drop Mrs Nuttall off at St. Thomas's Hospital?"

"Not on my route," Joe pointed out.

"Yes. But it's her baby. She has to get to the hospital urgently."

Just then Mrs Nuttall said "Oh, oh, oh! Please hurry," because her baby seemed very anxious to be born, even though it was foggy, and even though they were on the Flying 19.

"But the Professor . . ." Joe said. He was in a quandary.

"Professor," Sidi said. "Do you mind if

we drop in on St. Thomas's Hospital with Mrs Nuttall?"

"What for?" the Professor said angrily.

"She's going to have a baby," Sidi said. "Any minute."

"Oh! Oh!" The Professor was frightened of babies because he was always afraid someone would drop them. "Oh. Then hurry. Good heavens. A baby." The Professor ran up and down the bus and Mr

Nuttall tried to calm him and comfort him, but he was very worried. "Hurry, Joe," he shouted. "Use the Unlimited Emergency System."

Sidi suddenly remembered the twins. "You two are going to be late for school," she said to them sharply. "Do you want to get off?"

"Oh no!" the twins said. "This is much too exciting."

"All right. Fares, please," Sidi said and rang the bell and collected fares from the Professor and Mr Nuttall and Mrs Nuttall and the twins as Joe turned right at where Battersea Bridge would be if he could have seen it. He flew on in pitch darkness, in black fog, right down the river towards St. Thomas's Hospital.

The twins were so excited by now that they had, for the first time in years, forgotten their argument about the number of birds in the world. Instead they were now arguing seriously about who had stopped believing in Father Xmas first, and they got farther and farther back until Jix said that she had stopped believing in Father Xmas one day before she was born: D Day minus One.

Sidi was shocked. "How can you not believe in Father Xmas?" she said to them. "Stop that sort of talk this minute."

"But . . ."

"Not another word," Sidi insisted.

"But I was only going to suggest," Jax said, "that we ask the Professor if there is a Father Xmas or not. He knows everything."

This was an interesting subject and it kept their minds off the problem of where they were because Mrs Nuttall was begging Joe to hurry even though he couldn't see anything. They could not see a hand in front of them, and they couldn't even see Joe in his driver's cabin, and the bus

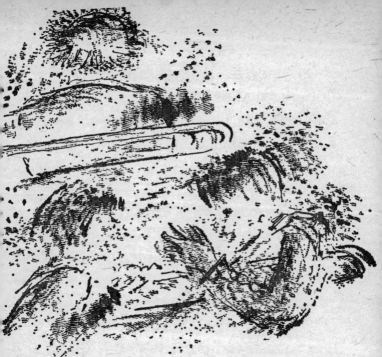

was so full of fog now that they couldn't even see each other. But the twins went on arguing hammer-and-tongs until Sidi said angrily: "Oh, but *stop* it this instant. Ask the Professor, for heaven's sake."

"Professor," Jix said. "Is there a Father Xmas?"

"Or is there *not* a Father Xmas?" Jax said.

"How perfectly disgusting to ask a question like that of an old man like me," the Professor said angrily. "Did you ever see a double-decker, flying, London bus?"

"Of course."

"Then how dare you question Father Xmas. I invented his airborne sled."

"Oh, thank you very much, Professor," the twins said, very pleased to be so wrong.

"Aren't you silly!" Sidi said to them.

Then a terrible thing happened. There was a crash and the whole bus shook and tipped and lurched and everybody screamed and Joe went *pum pum pum pum pum*!

"What was that?"

"We hit Chelsea Bridge," Mr Nuttall suggested nervously.

"Don't be silly," the Professor said.

"We hit something," Sidi said.

"Joe. What happened?" they shouted.

"Swan," Joe said. "Hit forward up controls, Professor."

"Are you all right?"

"Having a bit of trouble." *Pum, pum.*

Mrs Nuttall suddenly said "Oh", her baby was going to be born any minute and Sidi said: "Hurry, Joe."

"Doing my best." *Pum pum.*

The Flying 19 seemed to be twisting about a bit, and they felt as if they were going down. Then they heard a splash. They had actually touched the river. Joe fiddled with the Atomatic Adjuster and they got off the river and Joe shouted: "I think we're flying under Chelsea Bridge."

"Get her up," the Professor said.

The twins began to argue about how high it was under Chelsea Bridge. Jix said it was impossible for a bus to go under it, Jax said it was normal and logical and an everyday possibility.

"Oh dear . . ." Mrs Nuttall said.

Her baby was being very insistent.

Then they felt the bus go UP and UP. They felt their stomachs somewhere on the bottom of the bus just like going up in a lift. Joe was very calm, but he was struggling with the controls, the gears, the brake, the Atomatic Regulator and the UP controls.

Then they stopped in the black thick fog and couldn't see anything anywhere. They simply stopped, hung up there somehow, high in the black sky.

Joe knocked on the back of his cabin for Sidi.

"Sidi," he said. "Just step off, will you, and see if you can see anything."

"Me?" Sidi said.

"Yes," Joe said calmly. "Perfectly all right. Think I know where we are. Better make sure."

Sidi could not see anybody or anything and she held her hand up in front of her eyes and could not see it, but she bravely found her way to the platform of the bus, trying not to be worried by Mrs Nuttall's cries to hurry. And even though she was sure they were a hundred feet in the air, and that she would step off into nothing and disappear forever, she trusted Joe so much that she stepped off, although she kept a good hold on the side of Flying 19.

"High in the sky, in the sky, in the sky," Sidi sang bravely.

She found her feet on something solid. She knelt down and touched it. Brick. Impossible. They were hundreds of feet up in the air. It was hot. It was very hot. She began to roast. It was awful. It felt like some terrible place.

"Joe, Joe, Joe, Joe!" she sang. "It feels like a red hot hole."

"Thought so," Joe said. "Chelsea Power Station. Landed on the chimney . . ."

He had hardly said the words when the

chimney of Chelsea Power Station went PUM PUM and the bus was lifted two hundred feet in the air and everybody screamed and Mrs Nuttall said: "Oh, please hurry . . ."

The Professor was frantic. "Will you *hurry*," he shouted at Joe. Then he began to mumble to himself to take his mind off their predicament: "Have to put on an automatic swan fender . . ." And his mind worked busily on the formula as Joe got control of Flying 19 again and flew straight to the roof of St. Thomas's. *"Cf h by 3 to the x squared by f and two by seven t pie arred square."* That was the Professor's swan fender.

The bus came down. Mrs Nuttall was now sure her baby would be born any second. Joe couldn't see anything, but he knew where the roof of St. Thomas's was and he landed perfectly in the children's playground on the balcony outside Lilian

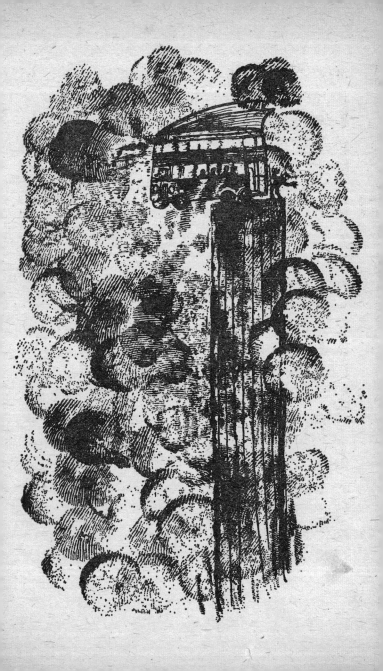

Ward, and when the Sisters ran out to see what was happening they couldn't see a thing but suddenly they heard talking and shouting and crying, and the twins found their way in and said:

"Please hurry. Mrs Nuttall is having a baby."

"But who are you?" the Sisters said. "Where did you come from?"

"The Flying 19 . . ." the twins said.

"Oh . . ."

Everybody knew Flying 19 by now, so that explained everything. They called in everything and everybody and Mr and Mrs Nuttall were rushed inside, and the Sisters invited Joe and the twins and Sidi and the Professor for a cup of tea in Lilian Ward but Joe said:

"Must get back. Don't know what London Transport will say to this. I'm very off route."

So they all got back in the bus and the

Professor said very nervously: "Thank heavens that's over," and he collapsed on what he thought was a seat. But because they still couldn't see anything in the fog it was really the floor of the platform. Sidi picked him up and said:

"Really, Professor. You know better than that. No standing on the platform, please."

Joe took off the No. 19 and flew around the Houses of Parliament, because he was afraid of flying over it in case there was another PUM PUM like the Battersea Power Station chimney. He dropped the twins off at Piccadilly where they went to school arguing about the size of Tom Thumb, and then he took the Professor on to the British Museum stop, and by the time he got back to Battersea Garage the fog had lifted and the CDD was waiting for him, and he said to Joe sternly:

"Joe! You went off route."

"That I did," Joe said.

"Well? Any reason?" the CDD demanded.

"Emergency."

"Your bus is damaged—left front UP control."

"Swan."

"We'll have to look into this," the official CDD said.

"Be glad to," Joe said gruffly.

"You want to look into what?" Sidi began, and she put up a good fight for Joe and herself. But they were both docked three days' pay and reprimanded for careless behaviour towards a No. 19.

Joe was very upset. "I never was careless to a bus in my life," he said. "Particularly a No. 19 . . ."

"Never mind, Joe," Sidi told him. "You're the best bus driver in the world . . ."

Joe was grateful to Sidi, but he was so upset with the reprimand that he said: "Don't feel that I can ever drive the old bus again, Sidi. Time I retired."

"Joe!" was all Sidi said.

But Joe just shook his head sadly, and walked away.

Chapter 4

NATURALLY there was a crisis. Nobody but Joe could drive the Flying 19. But Joe would *not* drive it any more, so once again everybody was jammed up in the traffic, and once again the Professor was so angry that he put his head out of the window of the Non-flying 19 and insulted every CDD he saw.

"How dare you!" he shouted at them. "How dare you treat the public in this way."

Insults never upset CDD's. They just smiled a friendly smile at the old Professor.

Of course London Transport were very happy anyway because everything was back to normal again. Everybody was late, everything was jammed up.

"All services and schedules are reduced as usual," the Public Relations Official said cheerfully to everybody who complained about the buses.

But by now all the world had heard of the Flying 19, and wanted to buy Flying 19s for their own countries. The Russians sent a lady cosmonaut to test it first because they didn't quite believe it, and the Americans sent two detectives to make sure a Flying 19 would not threaten America. But soon everybody was anxious to buy Flying 19s from the London Flying Bus-making Company who had built the first Flying 19 for London Transport.

So many people wanted to buy Flying 19s in fact that all the countries decided to hold an International Conference of Governments of the World to decide how many each Government would be able to have.

"This will make us lots of money," the Prime Minister of Britain announced on television. "It will save the country."

Jix and Jax had a fierce argument about why it would save the country, but the

Professor told them irritably that of course it was very, very simple. "Everybody in England is spending so much money," he explained, "that soon there won't be any money left at all. So we just *have* to sell something to get more money."

The trouble was that the International Conference of Countries of the World Anxious to Buy Flying 19s actually wanted to see the Flying 19 at work, and to have it explained to them. So the Prime Minister rang up Battersea Garage.

"Send the Flying 19 around to No. 10 Downing Street immediately," he ordered. "It's very important. We will build lots of Flying 19s and sell them and make lots of money. It will save the country."

"Sorry, sir," the London Transport Official said. "We can't send you the Flying 19."

"Why not? Hah hah. You're joking."

The Prime Minister was very boyish, like all Prime Ministers who go to school and decide never to grow up again. "Why not?" he demanded again.

"The driver is indisposed," the Official said importantly.

"Is what?" the Prime Minister said.

"Ill," the Official replied.

"Nonsense," the Prime Minister shouted. "I saw him yesterday in Battersea Park with his dog, cat and whistling canary."

The Official realized that his excuse was hopeless, so he admitted the truth. "I'm afraid Joe won't drive the bus, sir," he said.

"Why not?"

"I'm afraid we upset his feelings. We said he had been careless to his bus . . ."

"How silly," the Prime Minister said. "Well. Never mind. I'll ask him to forgive you this time, because we'll sell lots of

Flying 19s and make lots of money. It will save the country."

So the Prime Minister sent a special

messenger around to Joe's house to ask him to *please* forgive London Transport just this once, and to please drive the Flying 19 again, because it would make lots of money and save the country.

"It is your duty, Joe," the Prime Minister said sternly.

Joe knew he had to do his duty. "All right," he said gruffly. "I'll forgive them just this once. But I wasn't careless to my bus."

"Of course you weren't," the Prime Minister said cleverly. He always knew how to persuade people to do what they wanted to do.

So Joe went over to Battersea Garage and got into the driver's seat of the Flying 19, rang the bell, and they went off to pick up the Professor who would have to explain the bus to the International Conference. Joe and Sidi also picked up the twins, Jix and Jax, because the Prime

Minister thought it would be a good idea to have two Satisfied Customers to prove how good the bus was.

"Good propaganda," he said cleverly.

So Jix and Jax got a special day off from school which was a relief to their teachers because at their Special School teachers often went mad. It was the arguing. The teachers were so busy hurriedly looking up things in books, and answering hundreds and hundreds of arguments every five minutes (such as how heavy is a mosquito, and is the sky flat or round or oval, and hundreds of other fascinating questions like that) that they became quite silly from learning so much and had to be sent to rest at a school where pupils didn't know anything and didn't argue at all.

"Fares, please," Sidi sang. She was happy again, she was always happiest with Joe and the Flying 19.

Everybody paid their fare, and when

the Flying 19 got near Hyde Park Corner the traffic jam was so huge that Joe took her UP and flew by Buckingham Palace, avoided Parliament, and landed safely in Downing Street outside No. 10 where the International Conference was waiting for it.

Everybody cheered.

"Wonderful!" the Prime Minister of France said. "Formidable."

"Congratulations," the Prime Minister of Miridon said to Joe and shook his hand vigorously while the photographers took pictures and the television cameras made a film.

Everybody asked Joe lots of important questions. Had he gone to school? What age was he when he first ate a boiled egg? How many pairs of shoes did he own?

Joe gave very good answers. "Yes. Four. Two . . ." he said.

Everybody cheered Joe and everybody

watching television was pleased and thought how clever the interviewer was for asking such brilliant questions.

"Time to go," Joe said then.

"All aboard," Sidi ordered.

Everyone piled into the bus. The Professor had been asleep through everything because he thought it was night, and he was very annoyed when the bus began to fill up with noisy Prime Ministers from all over the world. The top deck soon filled, then the bottom deck, but four Prime Ministers were left standing.

"No standing inside the bus, please," Sidi said sharply.

"But there aren't any more seats, Sidi," the Prime Minister of Lower Sobli-sobli said.

"Can't help that. No standing," Sidi said. "You'll have to get off the bus."

Our Prime Minister laughed boyishly and tried to persuade Sidi to let them stand, but Sidi would not ring her bell until there was nobody standing, so the Prime Ministers of Lower Sobli-sobli, France, Germany, and Mongolia were turfed off the bus and Sidi rang the bell and everybody cheered as Joe took her UP.

UP they went over Whitehall, and the Prime Minister announced to the Prime Ministers of the World: "Our first call will be St. Thomas's Hospital where we will meet our first Satisfied Customer, Mrs Nuttall . . ."

Everybody cheered.

"Fares, please," Sidi said.

"Hah hah," our Prime Minister said to Sidi. "You don't mean it."

"Mean what?" Sidi said indignantly. "Fares, please," she said firmly.

"But good heavens," our Prime Minister said to Sidi. "We don't have to pay fares."

"Of course you do," Sidi said. "You can't travel on a London Transport bus without paying your fare."

"But . . ."

"If you don't pay your fare I'll have to put you off the bus," Sidi told him sharply.

"But, Sidi, I'm the Prime Minister."

"Can't help that," Sidi said. "Fares, please."

"But I haven't got any money on me," the Prime Minister said.

"What?" Sidi said in amazement. "You actually get on a London bus without having any money to pay the fare?"

"But Prime Ministers never carry money."

"What a terrible thing to say," Sidi replied. "Only the Queen doesn't carry money. Prime Ministers *should carry money*!" Sidi said angrily.

"I'm sorry," the Prime Minister said,

and he had to ask his neighbour, the Prime Minister of India, if he could borrow fifty pence but he had no money either. None of the Prime Ministers had any money, so Sidi was very upset.

"I'll have to take all your names and addresses," she said, and she went around taking the names and addresses of the Prime Minister of Britain, the Prime Minister of India, Canada, Norway, and all the other countries in the world.

"Hold tight," Sidi said then.

They were coming down over St. Thomas's Hospital, and Joe made a perfect landing on the balcony near Lilian Ward where the Nurses and Sisters ran out with flowers for the Prime Ministers of the World and welcomed them with Official cups of tea.

"And here's Mrs Nuttall, our first Satisfied Customer," the Prime Minister said proudly.

"Don't forget the baby," the twins whispered.

"Oh. And, of course, Master Nuttall."

Mrs Nuttall, the young lady char, was

very shy, but she showed off her lovely ten-pound baby named Joe, after Joe, who blushed and went *pum pum* because he was so surprised.

"Are you a Satisfied Customer, Mrs Nuttall?" the Prime Minister asked Officially.

"Oh yes. Joe's a lovely baby," Mrs Nuttall said.

"No, no, no, no!" The Professor had finally awakened and he got out of the bus. "With the bus, Mrs Nuttall. You must speak clearly. These people don't speak any English."

"Oh yes, the bus was wonderful," Mrs Nuttall said. "It was an awful day, terribly foggy, I wouldn't have got there if it hadn't been for Joe and Sidi and the Flying 19. My baby might have been born somewhere else . . ."

Everybody cheered and Mrs Nuttall blushed.

"Well, gentlemen," the Prime Minister said. "Let us continue."

They all got back into the bus again, Sidi rang the bell and Joe flew them over all the jammed-up traffic of London: up the Strand, through the City, down Cheapside, Holborn, Oxford Street, and Marble Arch. The traffic was all jammed up and nothing was moving more than the usual inch an hour, except the Flying 19.

The Prime Ministers of the world were all as happy as schoolboys.

"Twelve o'clock, twelve o'clock, twelve o'clock," Sidi sang.

"Oh dear," the Prime Minister said.

"What's the matter?" the other Prime Ministers asked.

"Time's up," the Prime Minister said.

Joe took them all back to No. 10 Downing Street where he landed very gently next to the policeman who saluted the Prime Ministers. The Prime Ministers

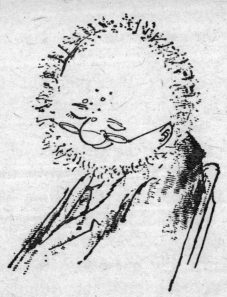

were very sad that it was all over and tried
to persuade Joe to fly them round London
once more, but Joe was a serious man.

"Shift finishes at twelve," he said to
them.

"Oh well, never mind," said our clever
Prime Minister to his friends. "You have
all seen enough, gentlemen, to convince
you that the Flying 19 is a wonderful
invention. A miracle, Professor . . ."

But the Professor was nowhere in sight.

"Where is he?" the Prime Minister said unhappily. "I wanted him to explain how the bus worked."

"He's asleep on the front seat," the twins said and went inside and woke the Professor and told him the Prime Minister wanted him to explain how the Flying 19 worked.

"What a silly question," the Professor said. "You just push the Atomatic Adjuster and that's all." And he went back to sleep again.

"But that's much too simple to understand," the Prime Ministers said and woke up the Professor again and said to him: "Please, Professor, couldn't you explain something a little more complicated?"

"No," the Professor said firmly and went back to sleep.

"Oh dear. Then we'll have to depend on

our experts," the Prime Ministers of the world remarked to each other in a buzz of excitement.

"Never mind," our Prime Minister said cleverly. "Now you may question our other Satisfied Customers—our friends Jix and Jax. Are you satisfied with the Flying 19, my young friends?" the Prime Minister asked cleverly.

"Of course," the twins said together, and it was the first time in their lives they had ever agreed. "We are always early for school, and we don't get punishments, and we are always home early after school."

"Hurrah!" the Prime Ministers said, because they knew what a problem getting to and from school on time was in their own countries.

"What do you find best about the Flying 19?" the Prime Minister of Switzerland asked them.

That was an unfortunate question because Jix and Jax began a terrible argument about what was best about the Flying 19, and Sidi had to take them aside while the Prime Minister made an important speech.

"Well, gentlemen," he said. "You can see what a fine bus Flying 19 is. It saves lives, it helps babies get born, it flies through fogs, it now has an excellent defence against swans, it does away with all modern worries, satisfies everybody who rides on it, keeps good time, is never in trouble, arrives safely at its destination, is silent, pleasant and easy to handle. So! Do you want to buy thousands and thousands of Flying 19s from us or not?"

"Yes, yes, yes, yes, yes," the Prime Ministers of the world shouted, each one trying to buy more than the others.

The Prime Minister made them all line up, and he took out his notebook, called to the representative of the London Flying Bus-making Company, and then took their orders. In half-an-hour the Prime Ministers of the world had bought £340,000,456.48 worth of Flying 19s. Split in half, this made £170,000,228.24 each for the British Government and the London Flying Bus-making Company.

Everybody cheered.

The Prime Minister, with tears in his eyes, thanked the Professor and Joe and Sidi and said: "You have saved the country. You shall be rewarded!"

They all shook hands with the Professor (who was annoyed because they woke him up again) and Joe and Sidi. Then Sidi leapt smartly on to the platform and said, "Stand clear, please," and rang the bell twice and the Flying 19 took off and went UP. They flew over all the Prime Ministers who waved, and Jix and Jax settled down to argue all the way back to Battersea about which Prime Minister had the biggest feet.

And that was how the Professor and Joe and Sidi and the Flying 19 saved the country. Their promised reward was a huge box of chocolates each, which of course they thoroughly enjoyed. Joe was so pleased that he agreed to drive the Flying 19 again on the regular route, and they were a happy bus again and Sidi sang all day and the *regularos* were on time again, and everything was fine until . . .

Chapter 5

SOMETHING awful happened.
An Official Inspector from the Ministry of Air Space called on Joe at his home and asked some serious questions.

"Do you have a flying licence?" was the first one.

"No," Joe said. "Driving Licence."

"Do you have Permit No. 121 to Navigate Flying Objects in or near or in the vicinity of London Air Space?"

"No. Driving Licence," Joe repeated.

"Do you have," the Official Inspector said more and more Officially, "Permit No. 4590 (b) to fly without a co-pilot in the vicinity of London Air Space?"

"No. Driving Licence," Joe said patiently.

"Do you have Aeronautics Flight Plan

Landing and Take-off Permits and Blind Flying Licence B and Radar Rating?"

Joe scratched his head. "No. Driving Licence," he muttered grimly.

The Official Inspector went through a long list of similar questions, and Joe replied very properly to all of them; but finally the Official Inspector said: "You are breaking the law, Joe."

"Me? Never broke the law in my life."

"You can't fly unless you have a Pilot's Licence," the Official Inspector said. "You will be summoned at the District Court on Wednesday. In the meantime you are not allowed to fly the Flying 19 again."

Pum pum pum pum pum pum! Joe was very upset.

Then the Official Inspector went to Sidi's house and asked her if she had assisted in Flying No. 19.

"I take the fares," Sidi said very angrily. "What's the matter with that?"

"You are taking money against the law," the Official Inspector told her. "Do you have a licence to collect money on a flying machine, Sidi?"

"No, but . . ."

"Do you have Permit 456 (a) to charge passengers on a flying machine for hire and reward?"

"Of course not. I'm a bus conductress," Sidi said, "and I don't know anything about Permit 456 (a)."

"Then you're breaking the law," the Official Inspector said and told Sidi that she too would be summoned with Joe at the District Court on Wednesday. "Please be there on time," he said. "In the meantime you are not allowed to conduct on Flying 19 again."

Sidi was furious and slammed the door in the Official Inspector's face.

But there was no doubt about it. Joe and Sidi had broken the law. The Flying

19 had also broken the law—even more than Joe and Sidi. The fact that all three were ignorant of the law, the Judge said, was no excuse. Of course, their friend, the Prime Minister, came down to the court and pointed out that the Flying 19 had now earned the country £620,000,000, and had saved the country. In fact, every country in the world now had hundreds and hundreds of Flying 19s.

"I can't help that," the Judge said to the Prime Minister. "The law is the law. I'm very sorry, of course, but the law says buses are not allowed to fly."

There was a big protest from everybody in court.

All the *regularos* of Flying 19 were in court, including the twins who had taken a special day off from school in case they could help and were arguing fiercely about whether the Judge was bald or not under his wig.

"Think of the time Flying 19 saves us," someone shouted. "It's always on time."

Mrs Nuttall was also there with baby Joe and she said: "My baby might have been born just anywhere, if it hadn't been for Flying 19."

Friends who had never even flown in Flying 19 came from all over London and said how nice it was, when everybody was jammed up in London traffic moving the usual inch an hour, to see Flying 19 soaring gracefully overhead in Joe's careful hands, always on time.

"*Don't take the wings off Flying No. 19!*" everybody shouted at once.

"Order! Order!" the Judge said. "I can't have these demonstrations in my court. If there is any more noise I will clear the court of everyone. Silence, please."

Everybody stopped talking.

"I will now give my verdict," the Judge said.

Everybody waited with bated breath. "The law is the law," the Judge said. "I don't make it. I can't help it. But there it is."

And he fined Joe £22.50 for flying without a licence, and forbade him ever to fly a Flying 19 again. And Flying 19 was forbidden to take off ever again, because it was against the law. And Sidi was fined £1.57 for helping to break the law, and she was forbidden to collect money ever again on Flying 19.

Sidi wept bitter tears.

"Where is the Professor?" everybody shouted when the Judge announced the verdict. "He'll be heartbroken."

Everybody marched from the District Court to the Professor's house to tell him how sorry they were. He was very surprised to see such a big crowd of people outside his house, and he invited them all in for tea. But of course they wouldn't fit.

"Dear, dear," Esmeralda said. "I'd better go down the street and buy some cakes. I wasn't expecting guests."

"Never mind, Esmeralda," everybody shouted. "We won't stay for tea. We just wanted to ask the Professor what he can do about it."

"About what?" the Professor said irritably.

"About Flying 19!" everybody shouted.

"What's the matter with it?"

"The Judge says it is not allowed to fly any more," everybody shouted out sadly.

"Nonsense," the Professor said. "What a silly thing to say."

"But it's true!" Sidi told him, still weeping sadly.

"Joe," the Professor said. "Is this true?"

"Afraid so," Joe replied.

"How perfectly disgusting," the Professor said. "I shall see about this in the morning. In the meantime, goodnight," he said to everybody.

"Goodnight, Professor," everybody shouted.

The next morning at the Headquarters of London Transport all the CDDs of London and all the Officials of Buses had a big Enquiry.

"We always knew it wouldn't work," the Head Controller of Difficult Bus Routes said.

"And you see," the Deputy-deputy Inspector Decontroller said gently to the Professor and Sidi and Joe, "we can't break the law, can we?"

"Flying No. 19 was not even a proper bus," the Chief Mechanical Official Deputy Ground Controller said.

"Not normal at all," the Head Official of All Late Buses said. "Quite the contrary."

They all pointed out that Flying 19 was

simply not right, it was simply not normal, and they really couldn't have that. "Everything must go back to normal," they said to the Professor.

"You mean no more Flying 19?" Sidi said angrily.

"No more Flying 19," the Officials all said together and began to cheer each other with the good news, because Flying 19 had given them such a lot of trouble, it had always been on time and was never in a traffic jam and everybody had loved it.

"Oh, very well," the Professor said. "I'm so disgustingly fed up I don't care what happens to your silly buses any more," and he left them all looking very pleased with themselves.

And that was the end of the Flying 19, which never flew again but was sold to a scrap iron merchant from Brixton who bought it for 58 pence.

Everybody was sad on the Un-flying 19s after that, in fact, all the people in all the London buses in all the traffic jams would sometimes look up at the sky and sigh. They longed to see one happy bus again.

Of course the Professor got angrier and angrier again because he was always late, and the twins got more and more punishments because they were always late, and Sidi didn't sing any more, and Joe gave up smoking his pipe.

In fact the whole story of Flying 19 would have ended very sadly indeed if Sidi didn't have a wonderful idea. One day she said to the Professor: "Professor! I have a good idea!"

"About what?" he said. "Don't bother me."

"About Flying No. 19," Sidi said.

"Don't waste my time, Sidi," the Professor said huffily. "The law says it is not allowed. No more Flying 19s."

"Yes, but what if the law can't see the Flying 19?" Sidi said.

"What do you mean?"

"Can't you invent an Invisible Flying 19, Professor?" Sidi said breathlessly.

"An Invisible Flying 19?"

"Yes."

"Invisible . . ." the Professor said.

"Yes. If it isn't there it can't be breaking the law can it?" Sidi said.

"Mmmmm," the Professor said.

Of course Joe was also very pleased with the idea but he didn't say anything. He was much too serious to influence the Professor in such things. But everybody else, including the twins, said: "Yes. Go on, Professor. You can do it . . ."

"Very difficult," the Professor said thoughtfully.

Everybody waited, but the Professor said nothing.

Then Sidi remembered something. "Oh

well," she said cunningly. "I suppose it *is* impossible."

Everybody realized then what Sidi was doing. "Yes, it's quite impossible!" they all agreed.

"Impossible! Impossible! Impossible!" Sidi sang.

"Impossible?" the Professor said angrily. "How dare you say that disgusting word to me. Of course I shall invent an Invisible Flying 19."

And that is the real end of the story of Flying 19.

I can't say whether the Professor actually invented the Invisible Flying 19 or not, because I've never seen it myself. But it has been noticed that Sidi sings again, Joe smokes his pipe again, the Professor isn't so angry these days, the twins arrive mysteriously early for school every day, and the young lady char Mrs Nuttall is going to have another baby.

Does this prove anything?

I'm not sure. But keep your eyes skinned on the London sky if you are passing this way, and if you do notice anything at all please do not tell London Transport, because if they ever discover that there *is* an Invisible Flying 19 they will then want to make *all* our buses invisible, and where would we be then?

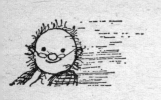

Nowhere of course!